This igloo book belongs to:

HArPer

Contents

igloobooks

Published in 2017
by Igloo Books Ltd, Cottage Farm, Sywell, NN6 0BJ
www.igloobooks.com

Written by Gemma Barder
Illustrated by Louise Anglicas

Cover designed by Lee Italiano
Interiors designed by Katie Messenger
Edited by Natalia Boileau

STA002 0717
2 4 6 8 10 9 7 5 3 1
ISBN 978-1-78670-672-0

Printed and manufactured in China

5 Minute Tales

Pretty Stories

igloobooks

The Best Dress

Jess and Amy were having a play day. They'd already pretended to be mermaids, fairies and pirates, and now they were looking in Amy's dress-up box for princess dresses.

Ooh! I'm going to wear this one,

said Jess, enthusiastically.

"But I want that one!" said Amy, looking cross.

That's the best dress and it is mine!

said Amy.

Well, I saw it first!

said Jess, snatching it away.

When Amy tried to grab the dress, Jess ran out of the room.

Amy ran down the stairs and chased Jess out into the garden.

"Give it to me," shouted Amy, as Jess ran along the path, clutching the dress tightly. Amy suddenly changed direction, **grabbed** at the dress and...

...Rip!

"Look what you did!" shrieked Amy. The girls had
tugged so hard that the dress had torn right down the middle.
"You snatched it," replied Jess, sulkily. "It's your fault!"

'What's all this noise?" said Amy's mum, coming into the garden.
She looked at the torn dress and was very disappointed indeed.

Arguing over
a dress? Oh, girls,
how silly of you!

said Mum,
with a sigh.

8

Mum could see how sorry the girls were and had a great idea.
She disappeared and came back with a box full of old clothes.

"I used to dress up in these when I was your age.
How about we brighten them up a bit?" said Mum, smiling.

Jess and Amy had a fun afternoon transforming Mum's old dresses.

There were reams
of ribbons and beads...

... and plenty of glitter, too.
The outfits looked **amazing.**

I'm Sorry I wouldn't
Share earlier,

said Amy,
feeling guilty.

Me, too,

said Jess,
hugging her friend.

The girls raced upstairs to change, and when Jess wanted to borrow a tiara and some shoes, Amy gave her the best ones.

"You both look wonderful," said Mum.
"Particularly **perfect** princesses!"

The Royal Fairy Games

The day of the first Royal Fairy Games had arrived, and Ella the woodland fairy was in charge of making the trophies.

We need terrific trophies for our wonderful winners!

said the fairy queen.

But Ella was worried. "What if I can't think of any trophy designs that are good enough?" she thought.

"I know," she said suddenly, "I'll visit my friends.
They're sure to help me think of something amazing."

Ella fluttered her wings and headed off to the enchanted meadow.

Lily the rainbow fairy was practising for the painting competition. Ella had just started to ask for help when...

Sorry, Ella. I'm too busy practising!

said Lily, dancing around and splodging paint on her canvas.

"Never mind," said Ella, fluttering off to see her friend, Rosa.

"Sorry," puffed Rosa the autumn fairy when Ella asked for help.
"I have cupcakes to make for the baking competition."
Ella's wings drooped with disappointment as she flew away to find Jasmine.

Jasmine the festival fairy was too busy rehearsing a song for the music competition to help Ella. "I'm never going to get any good ideas," sighed Ella, feeling worried. "The winners need trophies and I can't let the fairy queen down."

Just then, something fell on Ella's head and bounced
onto the woodland floor. It was a little acorn.

Ella stared at it and suddenly had a brilliant idea.
She flitted around, collecting as many acorns as she could.

Back home, Ella set to work.

She glued a chunky twig
underneath each acorn cup...

... then used sycamore
seeds for the handles.

Hmm, they still
need something
extra special,

thought Ella.

Thinking hard, Ella soon
realised just what would make
the **perfect** finishing touch.

Ella had some of Mia the stardust fairy's beautiful golden paint in her
craft cupboard. She added some pretty flowers and a final sprinkling
of stardust, and soon the trophies looked **incredible!**

Royal Fairy Games

Trumpets announced the start of the Royal Fairy Games, and the day was full of fun and cheers. The winners were **thrilled** to receive one of Ella's sparkling trophies, and she'd even decorated acorns for the runners-up.

At the end of the day, everyone gathered
around as the final trophy was awarded.

"I am delighted to present this to you, Ella,"
said the fairy queen, "for being Fairyland's most
creative, thoughtful and lovely fairy!"

Princess Amelia's Manners

Princess Amelia was used to having **everything** done for her.
She just had to ring her bell and someone would be there to...

...**brush** her teeth...

...**serve** her meals...

...and **read** to her.

The list was endless!

Ring!

Ring!

Amelia never said please or thank you. She didn't care that she was **spoilt** and demanding, she was happy that she never had to do anything herself. But things changed the day her sister Alice was born.

Suddenly, everyone was too busy to help.

23

"I can do everything for myself," announced Amelia,
as she **marched** into the bathroom one morning. But she
wasn't so confident when the soap bubbles went in her eyes and
toothpaste squirted into her hair instead of onto the toothbrush.

Next, Amelia tried to brush her hair, but the brush got caught in the tangles and toothpaste and ended up stuck.

Amelia's attempts at dressing herself weren't a great success either.

Feeling hungry, Amelia decided to make a big,
yummy breakfast in the palace kitchen.

But as she reached for the juice carton, she tripped over the cat,
knocked over the pots and pans, and sent cereal flying through the air.

I'm messy, I'm hungry
and I'm fed up!

she cried.

Feeling **miserable**, Amelia sat
on the floor and began to sob.

27

Amelia's loud sobs soon brought everyone running.
"I tried to do things for myself," explained Amelia.

"But I guess it's not as easy as I thought."

Amelia was cleaned up and given breakfast. "You're a big sister now," said the queen, "little Alice will learn lots from you."

I know one thing to teach her, said Amelia, with a smile.

"Being a **polite** princess is very important indeed!"

A Mermaid Tale

Beth and her dad were on holiday.
They built sandcastles...

... played in
the sea...

... and enjoyed yummy
ice creams.

Beth listened to the sound of the
ocean and thought how **magical**
it would be to be a mermaid.

Just as Beth was drifting off to sleep, she suddenly
heard a voice call her name. Sitting up quickly, she looked
over by the rocks and couldn't believe her eyes...

... it was a **real** mermaid!

The mermaid gave Beth a pretty shell. "Hold it to your ear and make a wish," said the mermaid.

I wish I was a mermaid, too,

wished Beth.

There was a **swooshing** sound and suddenly Beth had a beautiful, shimmering tail.

"My name is Melody," said the mermaid, taking Beth's hand. "Come and meet my friends." Beth flicked her tail excitedly and together they **dived** into the sea.

Splash! Down, down they swam through the crystal clear water.

Beth had so much fun with Melody and the mermaids.
They played hide-and-seek...

... braided one another's hair with sparkling sea jewels..

... and shared some delicious sea sweets

"Look!" cried Melody, suddenly. "The dolphins have come to play!"

Beth held onto the dolphin's fins, as they sped through
the water. The girls giggled with delight when the dolphins
swooshed through the water to make them laugh.

Soon, Beth heard someone calling her name.

That's my dad.
I have to go now,

said Beth.

Come and
visit soon!

said Melody,
waving goodbye.

"I will," called Beth, as she
swam up, **flicking** her tail until
she reached the surface of the waves.

Beth found herself back on the beach with her dad calling her. Had it all been a dream? Lying nearby was the pretty shell. Beth held it to her ear. "Perhaps I'll have more underwater adventures tomorrow," she thought with a smile.

Martha's Treasure Hunt

Martha stood in front of her mirror and **sighed.** It was nearly time for the final ballet show rehearsal and she really wanted to look her best.

I wish I had a prettier outfit, this one is so old,

sighed Martha.

That afternoon, Mum dropped Martha off at her class. She looked around at the other girls.

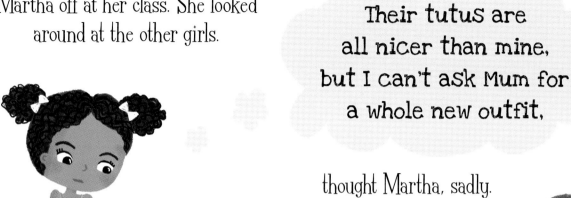

Their tutus are all nicer than mine, but I can't ask Mum for a whole new outfit,

thought Martha, sadly.

Back home after class, Martha found a note on her bed. It read...

Look under the bed, where you sleep at night.
I hope you'll be pleased and they fit you just right!

Under her bed, Martha found some **beautiful**
ballet slippers with another clue attached.

Excitedly, Martha read the next clue.

Now off to the bathroom to find Ms. Duck.
Look under the towel and you might be in luck!

Martha raced to the bathroom and found
a pretty, pink leotard. Where to next?

Down in the garden, you'll find a pot that's blue.
Hiding inside, is the next present for you!

Martha ran into the garden, found the pot and reached inside.
She pulled out some super sparkly tights. This was the **best** game, ever!

The next clue read...
Now think of the place where you watch all your shows.
There might be another surprise there, who knows?

"I watch my shows on TV!" said Martha, as she
ran to the lounge. Near the TV was a frilly tutu with a cute
satin bow. Next to it was a clue that read... Final clue!

Where is the bread kept? Take a look in there.
You might find something pretty for your hair.

Martha dashed into the kitchen
and found the final present. It was
a **stunning** crystal tiara.

She looked down at all the **amazing** things the clues had
led her to and couldn't believe that they really belonged to her.

Just then, Martha's mum appeared in the kitchen.
She looked very pleased with herself.

Mum, are these
all from you?

asked Martha, her eyes
shining with excitement.

Yes, you really
deserve them!

said Mum, giving
Martha a big hug.

"I know how hard you've been practising,"
said Mum, proudly. "Why don't you try them on?"

Martha stood in front of her mirror and did a little **twirl.**
"I love my new outfit!" she said, delightedly.

On the day of the show, Martha whirled and **twirled** gracefully across the stage. She had always loved to dance and in her new outfit she felt like a real prima ballerina.